THE LITTLE MARINE AND THE FLAG

CARISSA J. MARINE

TATE PUBLISHING & Enterprises

Published by Tate Publishing & Enterprises, LLC
127 E. Trade Center Terrace | Mustang, Oklahoma 73064 USA
1.888.361.9473 | www.tatepublishing.com

Tate Publishing is committed to excellence in the publishing industry. The company reflects the philosophy established by the founders, based on Psalm 68:11,
"The Lord gave the word and great was the company of those who published it."

Book design copyright © 2008 by Tate Publishing, LLC. All rights reserved.
Cover design and Interior design by Jennifer L. Fisher
Illustration by Eddie Russell

Published in the United States of America

ISBN: 978-1-60604-528-2
1. Juvenile Fiction: Family: Parents: War and Military
2. History: United States/Symbols, Monuments, Etc.
11.06.06

For Alex, Shelby, and Zack
with love and pride for your father.

Every morning the Little Marine wakes up to the sound of a trumpet playing. Jumping out of bed, he looks out his window over the trees to where his daddy works. As he watches, he sees a huge American flag being raised up a very tall flagpole. He loves seeing that big flag. He often tells his daddy that he wants to go see it and stand under it some day.

Early one morning when it was still dark outside, the Little Marine's daddy came quietly into his room and woke him up. "We are going to go watch the morning colors today, my Little Marine," his daddy said.

The Little Marine did not know what morning colors meant, but he was excited to go. Quickly, he dressed and climbed into the car with his dad. After a short drive, the car stopped. The Little Marine stared. They were in front of a very tall flagpole. *It is the exact pole the big flag hangs on,* he thought!

Stepping out of the car, the Little Marine saw several Marines standing at attention around the pole. One Marine was holding a large folded cloth with red and white stripes on it. The cloth looked heavy, but the Marine carried it strongly with pride. Suddenly, the Little Marine realized that the cloth was the big flag all folded up.

The Little Marine held tightly to his daddy's hand as they walked closer toward the Marines and the flagpole. Standing near the bottom of that tall pole, the Little Marine felt like a tiny ant! Squatting down, his dad whispered into his ear.

"This flagpole can be seen from anywhere on base. It stands over all the trees and buildings. The flag that flies on this pole is the flag of our country, the United States of America. This is not just a normal piece of colorful cloth. The first American flag was created many years ago under President George Washington. The fifty stars on the flag stand for each state in the Union, and the thirteen stripes represent the original thirteen states.

Watch how the Marine is carefully unfolding the flag, being sure not to let any part of it touch the ground. You must always respect the American flag. Never let it touch the ground, keep it from getting ragged and torn, and shine a light on it if it is to be flying in the dark. And you salute the flag by putting your right hand over your heart when you say the Pledge of Allegiance."

Just as the sun was beginning to shine rays of light into the sky, one Marine hung the big flag on the rope of the pole. While the trumpet played, everyone stood saluting the flag as it was slowly raised. When the flag reached the top of the pole, the trumpet stopped playing, and the sun was shining over the trees.

Returning home, the Little Marine was so happy to have seen the tall pole and the big flag up close. Now, every morning when he hears the trumpet playing, the Little Marine jumps out of bed and looks out his window. Placing his hand over his heart, he recites the Pledge of Allegiance as he watches that big flag be raised up the pole.

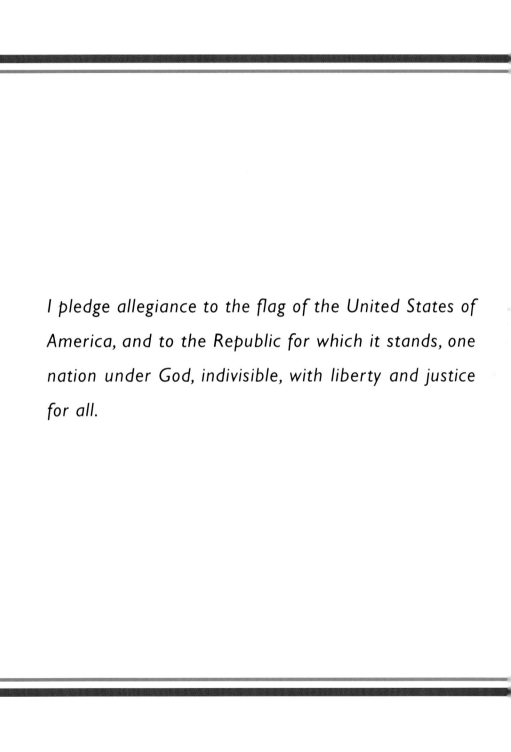

I pledge allegiance to the flag of the United States of America, and to the Republic for which it stands, one nation under God, indivisible, with liberty and justice for all.

listen|imagine|view|experience

AUDIO BOOK DOWNLOAD INCLUDED WITH THIS BOOK!

In your hands you hold a complete digital entertainment package. Besides purchasing the paper version of this book, this book includes a free download of the audio version of this book. Simply use the code listed below when visiting our website. Once downloaded to your computer, you can listen to the book through your computer's speakers, burn it to an audio CD or save the file to your portable music device (such as Apple's popular iPod) and listen on the go!

How to get your free audio book digital download:

1. Visit www.tatepublishing.com and click on the e|LIVE logo on the home page.
2. Enter the following coupon code:
   772b-53bc-c933-fbe0-c85e-01de-b8db-b8ce
3. Download the audio book from your e|LIVE digital locker and begin enjoying your new digital entertainment package today!